Read To
Your Bunny

This book

belongs to

Read To
Your Bunny

Rosemary Wells

SCHOLASTIC INC.
New York Toronto London Auckland Sydney
Mexico City New Delhi Hong Kong

ISBN 0-439-08717-1

25 24 23   4 5 6/0
Printed in the U.S.A.   23

First Trade paperback edition, August 1999

Book design by David Saylor

Reading together

twenty minutes a day

is the most important

gift you can give

your child.

Read to

your bunny

often,

It's twenty

minutes

of fun.

It's twenty

minutes

of moonlight,

And twenty

minutes of

sun.

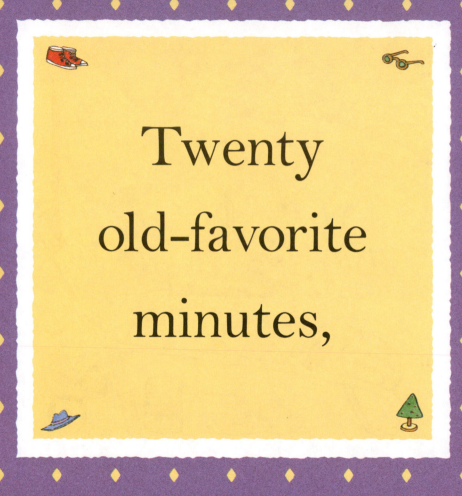

Twenty

old-favorite

minutes,

Twenty

minutes

brand-new,

Read to

your bunny

often,

And...

Your bunny
will read
to you.

ALL OF US love our children more than anything in the world. In their first years we feed them so they grow. We bring them to the doctor so they are healthy. We strap them in car seats so they are safe.

But the most important thing in the first years of life is the growth of the mind and spirit. This is when a child learns to love and trust, to speak and listen.

After a child turns two years old, these things are very difficult to learn or teach ever again. Trusting, singing, laughing, and language are the most important things in a young child's life.

And so they must come first for mothers and fathers, too. Because we can never have those years over again.

Every day, make a quiet, restful place for twenty minutes. Put your child in your lap and read a book aloud. In the pages of the book you will find a tiny vacation of privacy and intense love. It costs nothing but twenty minutes and a library card.

Reading to your little one is just like putting gold coins in the bank. It will pay you back tenfold. Your daughter will learn, and imagine, and be strong in herself. Your son will thrive, and give your love back forever.

— R.W.